IN THUNDER'S POCKET

IN THUNDER'S POCKET

Joan Aiken

Illustrated by
Caroline Crossland

RED
FOX

A Red Fox Book

Published by Random House Children's Books
20 Vauxhall Bridge Road, London SW1V 2SA

A division of The Random House Group Ltd
London Melbourne Sydney Auckland
Johannesburg and agencies throughout the world

3 5 7 9 10 8 6 4 2

First published in Great Britain by Red Fox 2001

Printed in Denmark by Norhaven A/S

THE RANDOM HOUSE GROUP Limited Reg. No. 954009
www.randomhouse.co.uk

ISBN 0 09 940483 4

CHAPTER ONE

I sat by the window, kicking my heels glumly against the dusty floor. When the train stopped at a station I didn't bother to look out – I knew that my stop wasn't for ten minutes yet.

But the fat woman opposite me collected up all her shopping bags and started to work her way past me. I pulled down the window and opened the door for her. She clambered out and went off, leaving the door open as

she didn't have a free hand to close it.
I was just about to pull it shut – rain
was blowing in – when a gull shot by
me through the open doorway and
started to hurtle about the inside of
the carriage, crashing against
seat-backs and luggage racks. Twice
it hit me – quite hard – and I could
see that it was liable to do itself real
damage if nobody showed it the way
out.

'Just keep calm, you stupid oaf!' I
told it; but it didn't keep calm.

My jacket was up in the rack –
Perdidas, black-and-white lozenges
with a black hood – so I snatched it
down and managed to loop the hood
over the frantic bird as it whizzed
past me for about the fifth time.
Bundled up inside the jacket I carried
it, kicking and flapping, to the open

window, and turned it loose. The gull shot off into the rain without a word of thanks. I slammed the door and shut the window.

The train began moving again. I flipped my jacket back into the rack and was about to sit down when a voice from behind me made me start – someone had come into the carriage from the corridor side.

'Hey – that was pretty neat!' said the boy who had come in.

He took off his own rain-spotted jacket and slung it up into the rack beside mine. It was the same colour. Then he sat down where the fat woman had been. He was about my size, brown-haired and freckled. He wore jeans, trainers and a t-shirt. He gave me a calm look.

'Where are you going?' he asked.

'St Boan,' I said. 'And don't I just wish I wasn't!'

'Thunder's Pocket. Oh. But why? You been there before?'

'No, never,' I said. 'Why do you call it Thunder's Pocket?'

'That's what the locals call it. Because they get such a lot of thunder storms. On account of how the land lies – a steep hill running down to a narrow harbour. Storms get trapped, you see, they go round and round.'

'I see.'

'Why don't you want to go there?' he said. 'It's not a bad place. Apart from the storms.'

'I have to go,' I said. 'Mum broke her leg falling off a ladder. She's in hospital. I have to stay with Uncle Adam and Aunt Lal. And I can't bring

Crowner, he's my dog, because the house is small and they have a cat. A *cat*, I ask you!'

'Oh. Bad luck. Still, it won't be for long, will it? And there's lots to do in Thunder's Pocket. You like surfing?'

'Never tried,' I had to admit.

'They run classes. You can fish, too. Your uncle got a boat?'

'I'm not sure. He has a shop – Readables and Collectibles.'

I asked the boy if he lived in St Boan, and he said no, half a dozen stops farther on. 'At Wicca Steps.'

I was disappointed – I had taken to him. There was something easy and sensible and plain-spoken about him.

'What's your name?' I asked.

'Eden,' he said. 'My friends call me Den.'

'Do you ever come to St Boan?'

'Yes, I do come sometimes – when I'm asked!'

There was a rumble of thunder overhead and a flicker of lightning over to the right where, now, I could just catch a glimpse of the sea, white waves breaking on a rocky bit of coast under a dark sky. The carriage lights blinked, went out, came on again.

'See,' said Eden, 'we're getting into the thunder zone. People who live in Thunder's Pocket have to manage without TV mostly. They get too much interference. And only a few have phones. Same reason.'

Good grief, I thought, what sort of a place am I coming to? And my heart sank another couple of notches. I'd been planning to ask if I could watch my favourite programme, Buccaneers'

Quay, which was due that night at half-past seven. I wondered if Uncle Adam and Aunt Lal even had a TV set.

They had a phone, I knew. I had never met them – this visit had been arranged in a hurry after Mum's accident.

'You watch much TV?' I asked Eden. 'What's your favourite?'

But no, he said, no, he didn't watch much. 'Only people! My hobby is collecting things.'

'Things, what sort of things?'

'Oh, fossils, shells. Puzzles. Numbers. Keys.'

'Keys?'

He smiled. The smile changed the shape of his face entirely and made him seem, for a moment, like somebody I half remembered from long ago.

Only, who could it be?

He said: 'Maybe I'll show you my collection sometime. The special thing about keys is that each one is made to open a particular lid – or door – maybe more than one. Yes, keys are very good things to collect. But look, we're coming to your stop'.

The train had slowed down. There were platform signs saying 'St Boan' and now the sea had retreated and lay far below us at the foot of a steep hill.

It looked like a black and wrinkled rug under massive purple clouds.

A man who must be my Uncle Adam, white-haired and white-bearded, was on the platform scanning the train as it slid to a stop.

'Well – so long – good talking to you. See you sometime,' said Eden as I hurriedly dragged my zip-bag down from the rack. 'Maybe we'll meet again one of these days. Hey, don't forget your jacket!'

CHAPTER TWO

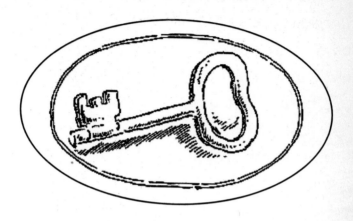

Uncle Adam, for it must be he, had already spotted me and opened the carriage door. I scrambled down on to the platform clutching bag and jacket in my arms.

'This is all your luggage?' said Uncle Adam. 'I assume you must be Ned?'

'Yes, that's all – yes, I'm Ned ...'

I turned to wave goodbye to the other boy, Eden, but already the train was slipping away, he was out of sight.

'Better put the jacket on,' Uncle Adam advised. 'We've a ten-minute walk and it's raining again. Every single day but one this summer it has rained, and that day it hailed. Nibs doesn't like it one bit, do you, Nibs?'

I was surprised to see that Uncle Adam's cat was with him. Nibs was a small compact tabby wih white whiskers and dark brown ears.

'He comes with me wherever I go,' said Uncle Adam. 'You might give him a finger to sniff, just to get acquainted.'

'It probably smells of dog,' I warned.

Nibs flattened his ears as he got a whiff of Crowner the terrier on my fingers, but then he rubbed his whiskers along my wrist to show he forgave me for keeping such low company.

I slung my pack over my shoulder and slid my hands in to my jacket pockets.

Then I let out a squawk. 'Oh, cripes!'

'What's up?' said Uncle Adam.

'I've got the wrong jacket!'

'Are you sure?'

'It's the other boy's, his was up in the rack too. I had an apple and a ballpoint in my pocket – I don't mind about those, he's welcome to them – but here's something of his ...'

I pulled it out.

It was a brass key, slightly tarnished.

'He told me he collected keys. I'd noticed that our jackets were the same. But, when I got out in such a rush – Oh, blow it!'

'Do you know his name? Where he lives? We could phone...'

'I only got his first name – Eden. He did mention the name of the place where he lives – wait a minute – um – I've almost got it. Wicker something. Wicker Steps, that was it. Half a dozen stops farther on, he said.'

'Wicker Steps? He must have been pulling your leg. There's no such place.'

I felt as if Uncle Adam had emptied a pail of cold water over me.

'Are you sure? He didn't seem as if he were having me on.'

'Maybe you dreamed him. Maybe you fell asleep. I didn't see any other boy when I opened the carriage door just now.'

'But – if I dreamed him – what about this key? And where's my apple?'

We had been walking as we talked. St Boan was a tight-packed little town, all set on a steep hill sloping down towards the harbour. At the foot of every street we crossed, I could see white crests of waves and masts of boats tilting back and forth. A gust of wind blew rain in our faces at every corner.

'Cars aren't allowed in the town unless they are making deliveries,' Uncle Adam explained. 'There's a car park up top.'

I was still worrying about the jacket. How could I have made such a stupid mistake?

Uncle Adam stopped by a red door

with a brass plate that said 'Doctor's Surgery'. He didn't go in, but slid a plastic card into a slot in the wall beside the door.

I was a bit startled to see a plastic-wrapped red pill pop out of a tube and fall into a metal cup below.

'Your Aunt Lal's daily pill,' Uncle Adam explained, pocketing the pill and carefully replacing the card in his wallet. 'She takes it at one o'clock.'

'Every day?' But why does she only get one at a time?'

'It would be dangerous to have more than one.'

How queer! I thought. What sort of pill could be so dangerous? And what sort of illness needed such a pill?

Uncle Adam began to explain as

we turned down one of the steep streets.

'Have you heard of Malot Corby?'

I felt I had just heard the name somewhere, but that was all.

'Is it a man or a woman?'

'A woman. Your Aunt Lal's and your mother's cousin. Yours too, come to that. She's dead now, died last year. She was a famous artist who lived in this town. She painted pictures and carved statues – the town is full of her statues, you'll see them all over the place. Look up there.'

I looked where he pointed. We were now crossing the harbour front. It was a curved, cobbled promenade, protected from the sea by a low stone wall. Up to our left, where Uncle Adam pointed, among the slate-roofed

houses on the hillside, I could see quite a big green, tree-filled space, with white and grey objects here and there among the bushes.

'That was Malot's garden,' Uncle Adam said. 'Now it's a public park. It's full of her statues.'

For the first time I began to feel that I might come to like St Boan. The harbour was grand, green dancing water and a lot of bobbing boats. And Malot Corby's garden which seemed more like a small forest than a park looked as if it would be a good place to explore.

'But what has Malot Corby to do with Aunt Lal's pill?' I wondered why Mum had never mentioned this famous relative. But then she had said hardly anything about Aunt Lal. Didn't seem to want to talk about her at all.

'I was coming to that,' said Uncle Adam. 'I wanted to tell you before we get home. It upsets your aunt to hear Malot's name. Gives her a headache. We used to live next door to that garden. And your aunt had a quarrel with Malot about some lace. And, just before she died, Malot put a curse on your aunt.'

'A curse? Honestly, Uncle Adam? You're not kidding?'

'Yes, honestly.'

'I didn't know people really put curses,' I said. 'Not any more.'

By this time we had walked right across the harbour front. Gulls kept swooping and diving past us, letting out harsh piercing cackles and shrieks. They were huge, black-backed birds, twice the size of Nibs.

But they stayed well clear of him
and he of them, though I noticed he
kept a wary eye on them.

Signs here and there said: PLEASE
DO NOT FEED THE GULLS.

Now Nibs,who had been running
along the low sea-wall – he didn't
seem to mind the rain at all – jumped
neatly down and turned inland,
away from the water, along a narrow
street which bore to the right and
uphill, over a headland.

'Oh yes, people still put curses,'
Uncle Adam said. 'In fact several
people in the town believe that about
half Malot Corby's statues are
neighbours she had it in for, that
she turned to stone.'

'But that's awful! That's wicked!'

'So you see how important it is,'
Uncle Adam went on matter-of-factly,

'that your Aunt Lal gets her pill every day precisely at one o'clock.'

I had a million questions I wanted to ask.

How did Adam and Lal know about the pill – what did the doctor say who had prescribed it – why hadn't the other people, the ones who'd been turned into statues, know to use the pill – what had the quarrel been about, how had it started – was there no way of getting rid of the curse – why had Mum never said anything about it.

At that moment, Uncle Adam said, 'Here we are.'

On our right the houses had come to a stop.

A grassy headland ran down to rocks where waves were breaking in clouds of white spray. The houses on the left went a little farther, and the last one had two beds of red geraniums in front, divided by a short cobbled path and enclosed by a low white-washed wall.

'Only just in time,' said Uncle Adam, pulling out a latchkey.

The clouds above were now black as tar and the rain had increased from a drizzle to a downpour. Lightning shot down the sky like someone slicing a curtain with the point of a knife and a terrific crash of thunder rampaged overhead.

'In you go, quick!' Uncle Adam whisked open the door and walked into a hallway which was small and dim, because at this moment the overhead light, which had been on, went off.

A voice from the middle of this

instant dark said, 'Did you remember my pill?'

'Of course!' said Uncle Adam. 'And here's nephew Ned with a stolen jacket and a mysterious key.'

CHAPTER THREE

During lunch the rain stopped and a watery sun came out, silvering the white tips of the waves.

But Aunt Lal said, 'Better take your jacket whenever you go out, Ned. It's liable to start pouring here at any time. Besides, the gulls in St Boan are such fiends. They'd sooner drop a slop on you than snatch a sandwich out of your hand – and they are experts at that, too.'

I'd already learned this on our walk from the station. The gulls in St Boan excelled in the sport of dive-bombing pedestrians, swooping low overhead to spray us with their white droppings. When we arrived at the house I had found gulls' mess down the back of my jacket – Eden's jacket – which I had to wipe off with wet tissues.

'You'll soon get used to dodging them,' Aunt Lal said, as she helped with the mop-up. 'The Council put up all those signs asking tourists not to feed the gulls but they take no notice.'

I wasn't sure whether 'they' meant the tourists or the gulls.

Aunt Lal had a very soft voice – I could only just hear her – and an odd way of talking, something like a lisp.

It took me a while to understand her. She was friendly, but gentle and vague, with a slightly startled look, like a person who's had a shock. Her soft white hair was bundled untidily into a huge heap on top of her head. It looked as if it hardly ever got combed. And her wondering pale-grey eyes never stayed still; they kept roaming around, looking over your shoulder or up at the ceiling or out of the window. The house was quite dusty. Slip-covers on the furniture were faded and worn. Uncle Adam, I learned, did most of the shopping and cooking. It seemed nobody did the cleaning.

Uncle Adam was plainly very fond of Aunt Lal and treated her like something very delicate and precious that had been damaged. She, I found,

spent most of her time making lace
on a pillow, using a lot of bobbins
and threads. It was fine, fine cobweb-
by stuff, quite useless, it appeared to
me, but it got sent off, Uncle Adam
told me, to famous lace exhibitions
all over the world. Mostly Aunt Lal
did this in the front room, with the
window open so she could see and
hear the sea. Or, if the weather was
fine, which it seldom was, in the back
garden,shaded by four big apple trees,
all loaded down with apples.

'You can eat as many as you like,'
Uncle Adam told me. 'But only the
red ones are ripe yet. They are
Worcesters. The others are Coxes.
They ripen later.'

Of course I wanted to get in touch
with Eden to return his jacket and
have my own back.

But Aunt Lal repeated what Uncle
Adam had said. 'There's no such place
as Wicca Steps, dearie. Oh yes, there
used to be, in the seventeenth
century, about twenty miles along the
coast to the west. It was a famous
place for witches, and a lot of them
got burned by King James. And then
the whole village fell into the sea. It
was on the cliff-top and there was a
big landslide after the winter gales.
Your friend must have been teasing
you, saying he came from there.'

I looked in the phone book but
could find no Edens. Anyway that
was his first name.

As soon as lunch was done, I went
off to explore the town.

'You can't get lost here,' Uncle
Adam said. 'All you have to do, in
case of doubt, is walk downhill and

make for the sea. Come and find me, in the shop, around five o'clock. You'll easily find the shop, it's in Fore Street, halfway down on the right.'

The first thing I wanted to do was go back to the harbour and look at all the boats. Now the tide was full in and great green waves were bashing against the harbour wall, sometimes splashing right over.

Piers like crabs' claws ran out on each side of the harbour. You could walk all the way out to the end, but I thought I'd wait to do that till the tide was out – just now you'd get soaked with spray from both sides.

While I was leaning on the harbour wall and dodging gulls and clouds of spray, a red-headed boy shot past on a bicycle.

'Hi, Eden!' he shouted and was

gone, out of earshot before I could tell him I wasn't Eden.

I thought it was odd that he should mistake me for Eden, since we weren't alike. It must have been the jacket.

A gull tried to get its head in my pocket and I decided to move on. I walked into town. There were lots of small shops selling beach toys and boxes with shells stuck all over, and peppermint rock in every possible shape – false teeth and oysters and kippers and soap – but I didn't want any of those things. I went on uphill towards the park that had been Malot Corby's garden. I was curious to see it, and all those statues that might once have been people. Would they *look* like people?

Ducking to avoid another gull, I nearly bumped into a boy who was careering downhill on a skateboard.

'Yo, Eden!' shouted the boy as he shot by. 'You owe me an apple!' and he disappeared from view round a corner between two squat little stone houses.

Gulls and boys, I thought: they all seem to be waiting for me in this place.

I found the entrance at the bottom of Malot Corby's garden, which ran uphill on a steep slope enclosed by a massive stone wall. The wrought-iron gate had a sign on it: **Malot Corby**, *one of the most famous inhabitants of this town, lived and worked near this place. Her garden is open to the public in her memory. Entry to her studio is through the garden. Tickets to the studio are available at the door. Adults £1.00, children and pensioners half-*

price. Opening hours 3 – 6.

I opened the gate. It had an angry, rusty creak like the voices of the gulls overhead. I climbed a flight of damp, mossy steps and started to explore the garden.

Well, it was more like a jungle than a garden. There were big clumps of bamboo, tall magnolia trees, fuchsia bushes, twelve feet high smothered with drooping, dripping crimson flowers, huge sprouting lilies, palm trees with furry trunks like gorillas' legs, and roses of every colour climbing all over the walls and bushes.

In among all the greenery it was quite hard to find the statues. Many were almost buried. Some were made of stone, some of bronze or copper. The metal ones were green and

tarnished with damp, the stone ones
smothered in green moss or lichen.

Were they like people? Not a bit!
They were smooth curving shapes,
like tall toadstools or melting candles.

If they had once been people,
turned to stone by a curse, I felt
sorry for them. It must be boring for
them, I thought, in this green jungly
place. If I were to be turned to a
lump of stone or metal, I would
rather be dropped into the sea, where
the tides would roll me and smooth
me and, in the end, wear me away
to nothing at all.

I wondered about Aunt Lal. If she
forgot to take her daily pill, which
kind of statue would she become?
The stone kind or the metal kind?
I could imagine Aunt Lal as a smooth
grey weathered stone.

A well-used cobbled path ran steeply uphill through the middle of the garden – why did I keep thinking of the place as a grave-yard?

A trickle of water ran out of a spout in a rock-face up above and then escaped downhill beside the path in a series of pool and troughs. I tasted the water where it came out from the wall.

It was very pure and cold.

'It's called St Boan's well,' said a soft voice beside me. 'The birds love it.'

I could see that. Swallows and martins kept coming to drink from the miniature waterfall. They zipped past, drinking on the wing. A few gulls hung about up above – this was the only part of the garden where they did come at all, the rest

of it was too overscreened by trees –
but the swallows chased the gulls
away.

The girl who had strolled up beside
me said: 'Do you want to see the
studio? I'm just going to open it up.'

She was a tall girl in a long red
cotton skirt. Her feet were bare. She
carried a bunch of keys.

'All right,' I said.

I hadn't planned to go into Malot
Corby's workplace but Uncle Adam
had given me a pound 'for expenses'
so I had no real reason not to.

The girl unlocked a couple of doors,
took my money, gave me change, and
then leaned against a counter, looking
at nothing in particular, leaving me to
wander about as I chose.

The studio was on two levels, with
a ship's ladder connecting them. The

walls were covered with drawings, rather good ones, I thought, birds and skulls and faces and plants and foxes and skeletons all mixed up. On stands arranged round the large room were statues; some of them seemed finished, some not. Unlike the ones in the garden they had definite shapes, a chimney with pot, an outsize milk bottle, a fire hydrant, a golf bag, a letter-box, a grandfather clock – all made out of brownish stone. While I was wandering round looking at them another heavy shower beat down on the roof like artillery fire.

'You'd better stay in here till it's over,' said the girl. 'It won't last long. Isn't your name Eden?'

'No it's not,' I said crossly.

'A boy called Eden was in here asking about Malot Corby. He wore the same sort of jacket as you.'

'Well, *I'd* like to know more about Malot Corby,' I said. 'Could she really put curses on people?'

'I think so. And other people do too. If she didn't like someone, they often just vanished away. Of course, maybe they just left St Boan.'

'Uncle Adam told me she put a curse on my Aunt Lal. She has to take a pill every day or she'd turn into a statue.'

'Oh. Well. Yes – I did hear about that,' the girl said awkwardly. She seemed embarrassed. 'That was rather hard on your aunt. They lived next door then, didn't they? Your aunt used to spread out her lace to bleach on the lavender bushes in her garden – she makes lace, doesn't she? – and Malot had a flock of tame seagulls.

She taught them to do tricks in the air, and of course they dropped messes on your aunt's lace. She complained about it. And that made Malot very angry – she had a short temper at the best of times.'

'How did Malot die?' I asked.

'Well, that was quite queer. It was only last year. James Kinsie, he's the mayor of St Boan, he asked Malot to do a statue of a famous pirate who lived here two hundred years ago, Thundering Jack, his name was. Mr Kinsie wanted the statue put out on the end of the pier. Said it would bring more tourists. But other people in the town didn't agree with that, they said it was nothing to be proud of that Thundering Jack had wrecked dozens of ships and drowned a whole lot of harmless people. Malot didn't

take any notice, she had a great piece
of rock fetched down and parked on
the end of the west pier and she
started working on it there. The rock
was full of iron ore, it was a huge
reddish jagged lump.'

'What happened?' I asked, though
I thought I could guess.

'Well, one day there was a violent
thunderstorm, Malot was out there
working with hammers and chisels,
and a great jag of lightning came
down – struck her and the rock, sort
of welded them together into one
great black frizzled lump. You
couldn't tell which was which.
Everyone was horrified, they didn't
want the thing left there, as you might
guess. But a few relatives of people
that Malot had put curses on, they
did want the rock left there, as a

warning. While they were all arguing about that, another tremendous gale blew up and a huge wave washed the rock into the sea.'

'That's odd,' I said, remembering how, only a short time before, I had been thinking how, if I was given the choice, I'd choose to be a rock rolled and smoothed by the waves.

'Why?' asked the girl.

But now it had stopped raining and some customers came in, wanting tickets, asking questions about Malot Corby. So I went back into the garden for an hour. I strolled back and forth, up and down along the paths, wondering why in the world Mum had never talked about St Boan, about Aunt Lal, about Malot Corby. Then, rising up from some deep, lost pocket of untapped memory, there suddenly came back to me a little snatch of talk between Mum and Dad – on Christmas Eve, it had been, a couple of years ago.

'Are you sure you don't want to ask Lal and Adam over for Christmas, Twinky? Your own sister? It always seems so odd...'

'No, Tony. I just don't want to risk it – and Lal doesn't want to risk it either. If Malot knew, if she got to hear, she'd be quite capable of stretching out the bane, the ill-wish, to cover us and Ned as well. And with a child you daren't – and Lal knows that.'

'No, I see,' he said, and then as I had come into the room they fell silent. That was before Malot died, of course.

I climbed the ship's ladder to the

upper floor of the studio. Here I found a whole row of objects like ships' bollards, like milk churns, like harps, like vacuum cleaners, like double-basses. They were all made from polished grey metal.

I walked up to one, shaped like a shiny grey, oversized milk churn, and saw that it had a keyhole in the top. I had been wandering about with my hands in my pockets and at this moment my fingers in the left-hand pocket found a thin short smooth metal band with a loop at one end – Eden's key. Without thinking or planning I took out the key and pushed it into the keyhole on the milk churn. It fitted; the key turned. I tilted up the top of the churn – which was hinged – and saw, down at the bottom of the churn, a piece of paper with a drawing on it.

A drawing, a portrait of my Aunt Lal.

With the same dreamy, instinctive certainty I took out the drawing and slipped it into my pocket, re-locked the lid of the milk churn, pocketed the key and climbed down the ladder. The girl at the desk was talking to another lot of customers but she nodded to me as I went out.

'Hey – you left your apple on the counter,' she called and tossed it to me.

I was going to say it wasn't mine, but she ran off up the stairs.

CHAPTER FOUR

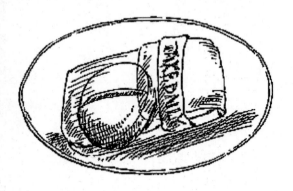

The church clock was striking five, so
I found my way to Fore Street and
Uncle Adam's shop. It was on a corner
with windows facing two ways. One
window was lined with book the
other had a muddle of brass pots,
china dogs, ships in bottles, wooden
shoes, and other things I could put
not name to. One thing I liked very
much was a spiral staircase about the
size of a footstool, made of bronze and

walnut wood.

'What's it for?' I asked Uncle Adam when I went in. He told me it was an architect's model and cost four hundred pounds.

There was a bearded man in the shop with Uncle Adam; they were plainly old friends and were in the middle of a game of chess.

'This is Doctor Mike Masham,' said Uncle Adam. 'He looks after your Aunt Lal.'

I was going to ask some questions about Aunt Lal and Malot Corby and the curse, and couldn't it ever be taken off, and what had happened to the other people that the sculptress had cursed, when the doctor's portable phone twittered in his pocket.

He pulled it out, said 'Yes?' into the mouthpiece and listened, and then

he said, 'Right, I'll be there at once,' and put the phone back in his pocket. He turned to Uncle Adam: 'It's Lal, Adam. That was Mrs Pollard, your neighbour. Says Lal's had a funny turn.'

'I'll go straight home,' Uncle Adam said hastily. 'Come along, Ned.'

'And I'll go with you,' said the doctor.

We went out – Nibs was there too and he ran ahead. The wind had got up and was blowing a gale. I saw Nibs flinch and put his ears back, then press himself into the angle of the wall as he scurried down the street. The doctor and I followed him while Uncle Adam turned to lock the shop door. Just at that moment there was a tremendous crash of falling masonry above as a whole chimney-stack fell into the street from overhead. The chimney pot broke off and bounced up from the pavement, catching Uncle Adam on the back of the head. He fell to the ground as if he'd been shot.

'Murder!' said the doctor, and he knelt by Adam and felt his skull. Then he pulled out his phone again and called urgently for an ambulance.

'I'll have to stay here with your uncle till it comes,' he told me. 'You hurry on home as fast as you can. Say I'm on my way. I'll be there as soon as I've got your uncle into hospital. If she's conscious, give your Aunt Lal this pill.'

He handed me a red pill in a plastic sheath, similar to the one that had come out of the wall dispenser.

'Uncle Adam's not killed, is he?'

I croaked.

'No, just concussed a bit, probably. Lucky his head's as hard as a bowls ball. I daresay he'll be sent home in a few hours. Now hurry!'

I looked for Nibs, who was waiting on a corner. By now the storm was doing its worst again – I could see what Eden had meant about storms going round and round in St Boan. Rain was slamming down, wind came in fierce gusts and thunder snapped and crackled overhead. Nibs hated it and I was glad Aunt Lal had advised me to take the jacket.

As I reached the bottom of Fore Street a flock of black-backed gulls flew at me. At first I thought they were blown by the wind, then I realised they were diving at me on purpose, striking at me with their

cruel, curved bills, whacking me with
their strong bony wings. I had nothing
to defend myself with except the apple
thrown at me by the girl in the studio.
I used it like a knuckle-duster,
bashing and thumping them, holding
my left arm across my face to protect
my mouth and eyes. The attack was
so sudden that I wasn't scared so
much as outraged and furious.

'Take that, take that, you filthy
bird!' I shouted, bashing one which
had its head half in my pocket.

'For heaven's sake, what's going
on?' said the girl from the studio,
who just then passed by with an
umbrella, and she twirled and twisted
the brolly among them until they flew
off with harsh angry screams.

'Thanks!' I panted. 'Mustn't stop,
my aunt's not well –' and I dashed on

after Nibs, who was crouched on the
next corner, hissing furiously, with
his ears and whiskers flattened. I
was glad he hadn't been any closer,
the gulls were so huge I thought Nibs
would be no match for them.

But when I got to the harbour
front I saw that Nibs and I would
have to turn back and take another
route. The gale had piled up the
water in the harbour so that waves
were surging right over the harbour
wall and water was sloshing about,
several feet deep, across the cobbled
walkway.

Nibs had already backed away at
the sight of water and now ran off
up a little alley called Sailmakers'
Way. Left, right, left, right, we
turned and twisted, while I worried
and fumed at the extra time I was

taking before I got home with Aunt
Lal's red pill.

At last I came out on the hillside
above Uncle Adam's house and had
to run down a grassy path beside the
garden. I noticed that the apple trees
were thrashing about in the high
wind. Apples were thudding down on
to the grass.

Nibs shot in through the kitchen
window. I went round to the front
door. The neighbour lady, Mrs Pollard,
was in Aunt Lal's front room, keeping
a look-out for the rescue party. When
she saw it was just me, her face fell.
I told her the gloomy tale of what had
happened to Uncle Adam and her
face fell even further.

'Lucky thing the doctor was right
there by him! But what'll happen to
your poor auntie? I have to get home

to my Jim, he's laid up with flu.'

'Is Aunt Lal conscious? I've a pill
I'm supposed to give her if she is.'

'No, well, she ain't, not to say
conscious, dear – more like somebody
in a dream.'

Mrs Pollard told me how she had
seen Aunt Lal, over the garden fence,
hanging teacloths on the line despite
the fact that it was pouring with rain.
Then she sank down to the ground.

'And just *lay* there! On the grass!
In all that rain!'

So Mrs Pollard had gone round and,
with great difficulty, persuaded Aunt
Lal to get up and come indoors and
lie down on her bed.

'But stay there, she won't, Neddy,
she gets up and wanders all over the
house. And her eyes are tight shut!
It's like as if she was sleep-walking!'

'Well, Doctor Masham's given me a pill for her. I only hope she'll take it.'

A thump on the wall and a loud call from next door now distracted Mrs Pollard.

'Nan! Nancy! Where are you, gal?'

'I'm a-coming, I'm a-coming!' she called back and threw me a slightly frantic look. 'You'll be all right now, won't you, dear, till the doctor comes? I daresay he won't be long. And we'll hope there's nothing much amiss with your uncle.'

I certainly did hope so.

Meanwhile I went upstairs and searched for Aunt Lal.

I found her in her bedroom, which was at the front of the house, its window looking out on to the grassy headland with its rocky tip and the white lashing waves that kept shooting up in clouds of spray. Hailstones big as fivepenny pieces now beat down out of the black sky. The ground was grey with them.

Aunt Lal stood at the window, but she was not looking out, for her eyes were shut. She held a pillow with a piece of lace, delicate as a spider's web, spread over it.

'But don't let Malot's gulls near it,' she said to me anxiously. 'Oh, those gulls! She trains them, you know, she trains them to do it. Brutes! They know what they are doing!'

'Aunt Lal, I have a pill for you here that the doctor has given me. Will you take it?'

'Pill, pill, no, I don't want any pill,' she said impatiently. 'There's been too many pills altogether.'

'But it's to make you better, Aunt

Lal!' I pleaded, hoping that Doctor Mike Masham would soon arrive with good news of Uncle Adam.

'What *would* make me better is a nice cup of tea,' said Aunt Lal. 'You make me a nice cup of tea!'

So I went down to the kitchen and made a pot of tea, hoping she might be persuaded to swallow the pill along with the tea. When I took the tray upstairs and poured her a cup she was sitting at her dressing-table as if she was looking at herself in the mirror. But her eyes were still tight shut.

'Here's your tea, Aunt Lal.'

I put the cup on the dressing-table in front of her.

'Thank you, dear. You're a good, thoughtful boy. Just like your mother. She's my little sister, you know.'

She took a sip of tea.

'*Now* won't you take the pill, Aunt Lal?'

'Not just yet, dear. I've such a headache. And those pills always make it worse. I'll tell you what would help, though.'

'Yes, what would?'

'It's just thinking of Malot brings it on, the headache, you know,' Aunt Lal confided. 'She's so wicked! She's my cousin, but we never did hit it off, even when we were tiny. She was jealous, you see, jealous because Twinky, that's your mother, and I got on so well with each other and Malot had no sister. Do you know, she once threatened to put our cat Nibs into her pottery kiln if he came into her garden. That was why we were obliged to move house. Just thinking about her gives me a headache.'

'Don't think about her, then,' I said. 'Drink your tea.'

She took another sip, eyes still shut, and said, 'What would help, would help a great deal, would be if you were to give my hair a combing.'

CHAPTER FIVE

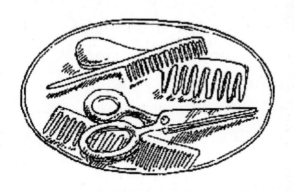

'Wow!' I said. 'That would be quite a job, Aunt Lal.'

Her hair, piled into a huge white mushroom on top of her head, looked as if it had not been combed for weeks, months, perhaps even years.

The very thought of tackling it made me feel weak at the wrists.

'Your mother would do it like a shot,' Aunt Lal said. 'Got a real knack, your dear mother has.'

This was true. Mother has her own hairdresser's shop in Abbott's Yarn and I knew all her customers must be in utter dismay at the thought of having to manage without her till she came out of hospital. When I was younger I used to spend a lot of time in the shop, watching the wonders Mum did with ladies' hair.

'I'll have a try,' I said doubtfully.

'Thank you, Neddy dear. You'll find a comb in the drawer.'

There were about a dozen combs in the drawer. None of them looked as if they had ever been used.

I started, as I had seen Mum do many a time, teasing out the ends of the hair, gently unravelling a millimetre at a time. It was no use tackling the thick tangled mass in the middle until I had all the ends clear.

And from the quantity there was
piled on her head I guessed her hair
must be at least a metre long – longer
than my arm – it might easily hang
down as far as her knees. I had to go
at it very, very slowly, holding each
tress tight between finger and thumb
so as not to hurt her scalp, while I
carefully drew out the snarls.

'It looks as if *gulls* have been
nesting in it, Aunt Lal,' I teased her,
not meaning to be taken seriously.
But she was angry at the very notion.

'That's what Malot would like!
That's what she wants!'

'Malot's dead now, Auntie,
remember? She's in the sea. She
can't do anybody any more harm.'

'No, but the harm she did still goes
on. That's the trouble.'

'This job is going to take me hours,

Aunt Lal,' I said after a while. I was anxious to get away from the subject of Malot Corby. 'Shall we take a rest? What would you like for your supper?'

'Oh, your uncle will soon come home and take care of that,' she said. But she did let me persuade her to get back on to her bed. No way would she agree to take the pill, though.

'No more pills. Never any more pills.'

I fed Nibs who was grumbling that it was long past his supper-time and then Dr Masham arrived, looking tired to death. He had gone with Uncle Adam to the hospital which was up at the top of the town, and there, he said, they had a couple of other emergencies waiting for him, someone who had been hit by a flying tile and someone who had been struck by lightning.

He shook his head when told that Aunt Lal refused to take the pill and tried to reason with her.

'You risk turning into a statue, you know, Lally.'

She was still lying on her bed, motionless, with her eyes closed.

'Well,' she said, 'if that does happen, drop me in the sea. But the boy's going to comb out my hair, and then perhaps my head will stop aching.'

Dr Masham sighed. 'Well,' he said, 'I can't compel you. I'd better help Ned make some supper. I could do with a bit myself. They are keeping Adam overnight in the hospital, but he's got nothing worse than concussion. Come on, young fellow, let's see what we can find in the larder.'

Downstairs, I told him about the key in my pocket, and opening the lid of the statue shaped like a milk-churn, and finding Aunt Lal's portrait inside. But, to my utter disgust, when I felt in my pocket for the picture I found nothing but some damp scraps of paper. I remembered how the gulls had pecked me specially hard on that side, in fact my left arm and leg were quite bruised and cut. Dr Masham gave me some stuff to rub on the sorest bits.

'It all adds up,' he said. 'The gulls were Malot's creatures. But just taking her picture out of that thing may have set off this change in your aunt. Keep on with the combing. If you can cure her headache, that's important.'

'In the picture,' I remembered, 'her hair was quite short.'

'She used to wear it short, just to her ears, when she was younger.'

We found some fish in the larder, which Dr Mike fried. But Aunt Lal would take only soup, which she sipped with her eyes shut.

'Even with my eyes shut I can see the lightning,' she grumbled. 'That's quite bad enough,'

The storm was still racketing on, round and round.

'Will you be all right here, Ned?' said Dr Mike doubtfully. 'I really ought to be back at my surgery and see a few more patients.'

'I'll be fine. I'll keep on with the combing,' I said.

'Yes, do that! I'll come round in the morning, as early as I can.'

When I'd washed the supper dishes I went up to Aunt Lal's room with a couple of apples I'd grabbed from the garden, by the light of lightning flashes, and proceeded with the combing job.

It seemed queer to remember that this time last night I had been in my own bed, at home, in Abbotts' Yarn. Now I felt as if I had lived in St Boan for months, for years.

Nibs came and settled on the end of Aunt Lal's bed. I had heaped a big stack of pillows behind her and pulled the bed away from the wall, so I could work first on one side, then on the other. She seemed drowsy, half asleep.

Every now and then she'd half-hum, half-sing some queer little rhyme: 'Line, twine, the willow and

the dee,' or, 'Intery, mintery, cuttery corn, Apple seed and apple thorn...' They made no sense at all to me.

I found canvas garden chairs in the back porch, fetched one of them upstairs, and was able to cat-nap in Aunt Lal's room from time to time, waking up every hour or so to go on with the slow task of unsnarling her hair. The lights flickered on and off several times, and finally stayed off. I found some candles and lit them.

The storm continued to rage. Rain slapped and streamed down the window panes and the whole casement shook with the battering of the wind. Beyond the wind's roar I could hear the thud and boom of the sea flinging itself against the rocks at the end of the point. And the voices of gulls, piercing and furious. I was glad to be ashore.

Around five o'clock, when faint dawn light was beginning to show, my work on Aunt Lal's hair was beginning to pay off. I had the back and side sections unknotted and spread out over the pillows. But there still remained a solid mass in the middle, on the top of her head. I had to tweak it loose, almost hair by hair. And it seemed to me that in the middle of this mass there was a kind of lump or bump.

This made me nervous. I worked at it very cautiously, very gingerly, in case Aunt Lal had some sort of swelling or growth in there which might be very tender and need medical attention.

You can guess how amazed I was when, under my teasing, probing fingers, I began to see and feel a white smooth something – and when, with endless care and caution, I combed all the matted hair away from this something, it rolled sideways on to the bedclothes and proved to be an egg.

Too small for a chicken's egg. I wondered if it might be a gull's egg.

But how in the world had it got in among Aunt Lal's tangle of hair?

And how long had it been there?

With this thought at the front of my mind, I took it down to the kitchen (Aunt Lal was asleep just then) and gently lowered it into a saucepan of water to hard-boil. I set the kitchen timer for twelve minutes.

Nibs had followed me down, and went out into the sopping garden.

I remembered Mum, in our kitchen

at home, saying: 'If you are ever in any doubt about an egg, *don't* break it, hard-boil it. A rotten egg is the worst smell in the world, and you can't get rid of the smell however much you wash and scrub and rinse. But once it's hard-boiled it isn't anything like so bad. You can just throw it away. And, if turns out *not* to be rotten – well, you can always use a hard-boiled egg in some way or other.'

I didn't see how this egg could possibly be fresh, not after months and months in Aunt Lal's hair.

How had it got there? Could some gull have nested on top of her head?

I put the kettle on a low flame, then went upstairs and finished off the job of combing. Aunt Lal's long, fine white hair now hung loose and

straight, like last night's lines of rain streaming down the dark window pane.

'Oh!' she sighed gratefully. 'That *does* feel comfortable.' And she suddenly scrambled out of bed to go and admire herself in the glass. Her eyes opened wide. Grey yesterday, they now shone bright blue.

On the floor lay a huge pile of combings and fluff and dust which I had removed from her head – no wonder she had a headache! It was enough to fill a large waste-basket. I had brought up a brush and dustpan and began sweeping all the heap together.

'Do you know what I'd like now, Ned,' said Aunt Lal, 'I'd like you to cut off all my hair, cut it quite short.'

'Golly Moses, Aunt Lal – wouldn't

it be better to wait and go to a proper hairdresser. I'm sure Mum would do it for you?'

'No, no,' she said impatiently. 'I want it done *now*. Go and look in the red leather bag in the front room downstairs, among my lace-making tools you'll find some sharp scissors with red handles. Your mother can style it for me later.'

So I hunted among the lace-making equipment in the room below and found an impressive pair of scissors with big round red handles and razor-sharp blades.

Then I checked in the kitchen. All was calm there. The white egg in the pan was bubbling away gently, the timer said three minutes to go, and the kettle was about to boil.

I made a pot of tea, left it to brew,

and ran upstairs again with the scissors. Aunt Lal had sat herself on her dressing-stool with a big white bath-towel draped over her shoulder.

'Quick, now!' she ordered. 'I can feel the weight of the hair hanging down all round me – it's pulling me down to the floor – starting another headache. Someone else might come and build a nest on my head. Just you snip it all off, between my ears and my shoulders.'

So I snipped. The blades were so sharp, it was like cutting through cobwebs, and the soft white masses of hair fell away to the floor in sheaves, thick as corn at harvest time.

'Oh, that feels *wonderful*,' sighed Aunt Lal, moving her head and shoulders. 'So light! So free! And now I'll tell you what I'd really fancy for my breakfast when you've swept it all up, a nice boiled egg ...'

Just as she said the word *egg* there came a terrific bang from downstairs. Simultaneously the window blew open on a wild gust of wind.

CHAPTER SIX

'Oh my dear heavens!' gasped Aunt Lal. 'Has the boiler burst? Quickly, go and see what's happened, Ned dear, but take care – I'll see to shutting the window.'

I ran down to the kitchen. I could easily guess what had happened, and I was right: the egg in the saucepan had exploded.

Bits of white eggshell were all over

the kitchen, and also little shreds of black feathers, bits of claws and beak. I didn't like the look of them *at all*. Whatever had been in that egg, I was glad it had come to no good. I was glad it hadn't hatched out on top of Aunt Lal's head.

But it was going to take hours to clear up the kitchen.

I heard a shriek from upstairs.

'Ned – help – help! Come quick!'

I dashed up again. Coming from Lal's room I could hear a violent flapping of wings and the raucous cries of gulls, dozens of gulls, from the sound ...

And in fact when I burst into her bedroom the air seemed to be entirely full of black-and-white bodies and yellow beaks circling and thrashing about, savagely pecking and swooping and snatching. Crouched in the middle of it all was Aunt Lal, who had wrapped the white towel round her head and shoulders to shield herself. The air was thick with white whirling hair and fluff as well. The scene was like an Arctic blizzard.

I grabbed the scissors in one hand, Aunt Lal's hairbrush in the other, and began dealing out bashes and stabs.

'Lie down, Aunt Lal!' I shouted. 'Lie on the bed!'

'Hair spray!' she gasped, doing so. 'Your mother gave me. On the bureau.'

It took me a couple of seconds to understand her, then I fought my way to the chest of drawers where there was a big red can with white stripes and a spray nozzle and orange

lettering saying that it was somebody's vitamin-hair-something. I had seen similar cans in Mum's shop. Plainly Aunt Lal had never used it for it still had a protective label over the nozzle which I tore off. Then I began squirting the gulls with the gluey, sweet-scented stuff, which got into their eyes and beaks and soon had them flopping on the floor in dismay.

As fast as they did so, I flung them out of the open window. At last there were only a few left.

Nibs came back just at this moment, damp from the garden and disapproving. One of the gulls dived at him, but he caught it in mid air, doing a spectacular leap and pounce, digging his claws into its back. His green eyes blazed with triumph.

'All right, Nibs, I'll chuck it out of the window,' I panted and did so.

Then I felt a sharp stab in my neck. The leader of the flock, the biggest bird, had swooped on me and jabbed me; now he skimmed up to the ceiling, hovered, and came fiercely down at me again. I still clutched the scissors in my left hand, point upward; diving down at me he landed full on the point, which ran deep into his chest. He dropped dead on the floor and Nibs, who had felt cheated when I threw his prey out of the window, gave me a warning growl and dragged the big gull out of the room.

I could hear it going thump, thump, thump, all the way down the stairs.

'Oh my dear Ned!' said Aunt Lal faintly. 'What a very lucky thing that you were in the house!'

'Well,' I croaked, 'I'm not so sure about that, Aunt Lal.'

What I felt in a vague muddled way was that if I hadn't come to the house in the first place, none of these things would have happened. But, to set against that was the undoubted fact that Aunt Lal seemed so much better today – quite well, in fact – brisk and clear-headed, and looked twenty years younger than she had yesterday. She even had a trace of pink in her cheeks.

But the house!

'You go back to bed, just for now, Aunt Lal,' I suggested. 'And eat this apple – look, I'm having the other one – and I'll do a bit of clearing up. Then, in about twenty minutes, I'll bring you a nice boiled egg. I'll just fetch the vacuum cleaner. You do have one, I hope? Then I'll give this room a bit of a tidy.'

The room looked as if a hurricane had hit a hair-shirt-and-feather-bed factory.

When, reluctantly, Aunt Lal had agreed to my cleaning programme – yes, she said, there was a Whizzo vacuum cleaner in the cupboard under the stairs; it didn't always work because of the thunder but perhaps it would today as the storm seemed to have passed over. I fetched up the Whizzo and cleared all the mess in the bedroom and stuffed the hair and feathers in two bin bags which I tied tightly and put outside by the garden wall.

The sun was trying to shine.

'Such a piece of luck,' Aunt Lal

said happily. 'It's Clear-up Day.'

Despite my urging her to stay in bed she had dressed and while I was hauling out the bags she came downstairs.

'Dustbin day, do you mean, Aunt Lal?'

'No, better than that. Every six months we have it, in St Boan. Anybody can put anything outside their house that they are tired of and want to give away – books, LP records, old clothes, furniture – anything – and anybody else can take it, if they fancy it. Then, at the end of the day, the Town Council picks up whatever is left, things that nobody wants.'

'And what happens to those things?'

'Well, I'm not quite sure,' she admitted. 'I suppose they are put on a dump somewhere.'

Aunt Lal did seem a trifle startled when she saw the mess in the kitchen.

'An egg with some black feathered thing inside?'

'That was what you had on your head, Aunt Lal!'

'No wonder my head ached,' she said. 'Malot must have put it there, some time when I was asleep in the garden – maybe *she* was in that egg herself?'

'Let's not think about it,' I suggested.

'But where is your uncle all this time? Where is Adam?'

So I had to explain all over again what had happened to him. She had clean forgotten what Doctor Masham had told her before. Then we began on the job of clearing up the kitchen.

Nibs had retired to the garden with the dead gull, but he soon decided that gulls were not a fit diet for cats and so I stuffed it into yet another dustbin bag with all the black feathers and claws. There seemed to be far more than could have come from one small egg.

In the middle of this activity a car pulled up outside and Doctor Mike got out escorting Uncle Adam with a bandaged head.

The two men were utterly thunderstruck at the sight of Aunt Lal.

Dr Masham kept walking round her, round and round, saying, 'I wouldn't have believed it possible! No; I wouldn't have believed it!'

Uncle Adam hugged Lal and kissed her and had to sit down hurriedly on a kitchen chair because his legs were still weak from his concussion. I boiled four eggs and made some toast and put on the kettle again for more tea.

'Adam, it's Clear-Out Day,' said Aunt Lal happily. 'Do you know what? I'm going to get rid of all my lace. I've made enough lace. I'm going to find something better to do. Perhaps I'll help you in the shop.'

'Get rid of your lace?' he said, astonished. 'But it's so beautiful!'

'No. I only made it to annoy Malot. Because I knew that she couldn't make lace.'

'And is that why she made statues?' said Doctor Mike. 'To annoy you?'

'That's a hard one,' Aunt Lal said thoughtfully. 'And I don't know the answer.'

I decided to go out and leave them talking.

The sun shone. It was hot. I didn't want to waste any of the fine weather.

I took down my jacket from the peg by the front door and pulled it on, automatically shoving my hands into the pockets.

And let out a yip.

For in one pocket was a key, and in the other, my apple and my ballpoint.

Perhaps, I thought, walking down towards the rocks, perhaps I'll meet that boy Eden again and he'll show me something else for the key to unlock...